T0114775

The Bird Boy's Song

Published by
Mzuni Press
P/Bag 201 Luwinga
Mzuzu 2

ISBN   978-99960-66-06-1
eISBN 978-99960-66-07-8

The Luviri Press is represented outside Africa by:
African Books Collective Oxford
(orders@africanbookscollective.com)

www.luviripress.blogspot.com

www.africanbookscollective.com

The Bird Boy's Song

Steve Chimombo

Luviri Press

Mzuzu

2021

Dedication

For Akubwalula, Akuchilawe and Akupherani, all mistresses of the art of storytelling, who passed on to me their art. They also understood only too well the meaning of this story.

Introduction

I grew up listening to the story of the orphan and the slave boy from several close relatives: my mother, my aunts, then my sisters. When I went to my mother's village, I used to sleep with my cousins at my aunt's place. Almost every night there was a storytelling session. This story would appear very often. However, the version that I recorded later was from Akubwalula. This is the version that appears in the Appendix.

My expanded version takes into account modern storytelling techniques. I had to supply causality, which was absent from the original story. This was needed in two important episodes, for example: why the orphan was sent back to his mother's village, and why the slave usurped his master's role in spite of being given and enjoying his freedom. The modern reader or writer worries about such details. The traditional raconteur does not!

Other aspects I expanded on were flashbacks and dialogue, as well as. description. These details were scantily supplied in the original. The additions supplemented the causality and enhanced the story, making it more plausible.

I had always called this story "The Orphan and the Slave." It was descriptive, but rather dull for a book title. In our storytelling sessions, we used to ask for *"Aah! Mbalame!"* ("Aah! Birds!"), but that would not be a suitable title for a translation. I decided to call the story "The Bird Boy's Song" because it retains the original idea and invites the reader to find out what it is all about.

Chapter One

The Orphan

Chosadziwa stopped suddenly. Dzunzo, walking behind him, almost bumped into him.

"What is it?" Dzunzo asked.

"Let's go back," Chosadziwa answered. There was something close to fright in his voice. He pointed, shoving his head forward at an angle and staring fixedly ahead.

Dzunzo, being shorter, could not see the object Chosadziwa was pointing at. The path was so narrow, he could not pass without brushing against the shrubs on either side.

"What is it?" he repeated impatiently, almost pushing Chosadziwa aside. He did not want his companion's fear to infect him. It had done so already, earlier that morning.

"Look." Chosadziwa stepped aside for his mate to come up. Dzunzo sidled up to him and followed the pointing finger.

"But it's only a chameleon!"

"I know."

"So what's wrong?"

"It means bad luck."

"What has the chameleon got to do with it?"

"We'll meet bad luck, either on the way or when we get there."

"We're almost half way there. We can't go back now."

"We've got to." Chosadziwa was trembling. "This is the second time omens have been placed in our path today."

"You mean the double-headed snake'?"

"Yes, I told you it means misfortune will dog us."

"We haven't met any ill luck so far."

"We haven't completed our journey yet."

"We've got to go on." Dzunzo shook his head vehemently. "What is there to go back to?"

Dzunzo's thoughts went back to Maitsalani Village, which they'd left a few weeks before. No, they could not return to face the same ill-treatment they'd suffered after his father's death. His uncles, aunts, grandfather and grandmother, who had seemed nice people before, changed their attitude towards him. His cousins' behaviour had also turned sour. Even his playmates had behaved as if he was a stranger to them. This had pushed Dzunzo closer and closer to Chosadziwa, who was really the stranger in the village. Chosadziwa was a slave his father had bought from some itinerant hunters he'd met near Maitsalani forest. His father, who had bought some elephant meat from the hunters, asked what was wrong with the boy since he looked so miserable in their company.

"He's only a slave," they had told him dismissively, as if referring to a piece of rotten wood not even fit for kindling.

"Can I buy him off you?"

"It makes no difference to us," the hunters responded. "We captured him in the hills way back."

"I'll give you two bags of sorghum for him."

The hunters accepted and abandoned their ward without qualms.

"Here's a playmate for you," was the way Dzunzo's father had introduced the new family member to his only son.

"What's your name?" was Dzunzo's overture.

"Chosadziwa," the slave boy answered diffidently, drawing lines on the ground with the big toe of his right foot.

"Where do you come from?"

"Beyond the hills," was the vague response, given with a toss of his head and a sniff.

7

Although Chosadziwa was several years older than Dzunzo, they got on very well. He fitted into the household easily. In fact, as soon as he'd recovered from the shock of being captured and sold, he seemed to fit into anything and everything around him. His charming manners, pleasant face, quick wit and movements, made him acceptable, if not companionable, to everyone. Dzunzo grew to love him like an older brother.

Dzunzo soon realised that Chosadziwa was also an inexhaustible source of information. He knew the names of most of the trees, shrubs and grasses around. He could not only name them but also tell what to do with them or what they were useful for: you ate the fruit raw, cooked the leaves for *ndiwo*, used the stems for building with or for medicinal purposes. He knew the names and habits of the animals, reptiles, birds and insects too. He knew how to trap the smaller ones, he made bows and arrows for Dzunzo and himself. He tapped *kachere* or *nkhadzi* trees for the sap to boil into lime for catching birds in the fields, in the bush, and by the riverside. Although Dzunzo was not in favour of killing any living thing just for the sake of it, he found Chosadziwa's talents and skills fascinating, if not worth emulating.

Ndasauka, Dzunzo's father, also grew to like Chosadziwa. There was no one else to share his parental love after his wife had passed away. He lavished it on the two boys without discriminating. Now, after his-father's death, Dzunzo also knew what the absence of love felt like.

It had started slowly, the cousins and playmates not calling out to Dzunzo and Chosadziwa to come and play. When Dzunzo and Chosadziwa went to the playground, they found the circle of their mates would only open grudgingly to admit them. When Dzunzo and Chosadziwa got up some mornings, they would find their playmates had all gone to the hills to collect *masuku*, *mpoza*, or *materne* fruit, without inviting them. Or Dzunzo and Chosadziwa would hunt for them only to find them at the riverside, bathing, washing, or just playing.

It then came out in whispers.

"We have received visitors," Dzunzo's cousins would tell their parents when he went to their homes.

"Are they eating with us?" came the testy question at meal times. "

8

"They didn't say."

"Well, go and ask them."

Yet Dzunzo and Chosadziwa had eaten at his cousins' homes hundreds of times before. Not only that, before his father's death, his cousins had eaten hundreds of times at his home. Dzunzo and Chosadziwa found this behaviour inexplicable.

"No," Dzunzo would answer firmly for both of them. "We'll eat at home. In fact, we're leaving now. Thank you."

Like an overstretched elastic band, the tenuous relationship between Dzunzo and the rest of the village threatened to snap at any moment.

"What are we going to do?" Chosadziwa asked Dzunzo. He too had read the signs.

"I don't know." Dzunzo was confused, almost in tears, shoulders convulsing, chest heaving with suppressed emotions.

"Don't you have any other relatives anywhere else?"

"You mean for us to leave this village?"

"Yes!"

"Leave my uncles and aunts, cousins, grandparents?"

"But it's obvious they don't want you here, and even less me, a slave, no relative of theirs."

"But where would we go? We're too young to go away and build a house somewhere else, where no one knows us."

"You must have relatives somewhere. Think hard."

More pressure came, from the elders this time, again subtly at first. It came in the form of *chitengwa*. The word was passed on from the elders to the youth, from cousins to playmates, like a hot stone no one wanted to keep for long.

"Your mother was a *mtengwa*!" The word came as a taunt, if not an accusation.

9

Dzunzo's mother, Nalichowa, had died when he was about six or seven. She had not taught him that word. Dzunzo remembered her as a very loving mother.

"You'll remember me when I die, my son," she would say sadly, as she placed a plate of *nsima* and *chisoso* for him to eat on the *khonde* at sunset.

"You won't die, mother," he would protest tearfully.

"Chauta knows we shall all die." She would return to the kitchen just as tearfully.

She died before she could tell him what *chitengwa* was. His father likewise died before explaining the word to him. In fact, he had never heard it from anyone's lips before his parents' death. Now it seemed the most important word for him to know.

"What is a *mtengwa?*" Dzunzo asked the elders who came to his father's house one evening.

"A woman who leaves her own home village to live with her husband in his village," explained Madala. "She makes the husband's village her home."

"What's wrong with doing that, then?" Dzunzo was puzzled. "The two love each other enough for one of them to sacrifice her own village."

"It's not as simple as that, child." Madala shook his head pityingly.

"Then explain it to me fully, so that I can understand."

"Your father had to pay a fee to your mother's people to be allowed to take her away."

"What fee?"

"We can't remember the details. It was a long time ago, before you were born."

"The fee can be anything," elaborated Mdoda. "A few heads of goat, perhaps cattle, baskets of sorghum, anything substantial."

"Why?"

"In return for not building a house in your mother's village, and other things."

"You see," Mdoda came to the rescue again, "a man is supposed not only to build a house for his wife, but also to hoe her garden for their food. He accumulates wealth which he shares with his wife's relatives and even the chief. When he dies, he leaves all this property behind for his wife, children and relatives to enjoy."

"What has this got to do with my parents?"

"By being a *mtengwa,*" Madala explained, as if to a moron, "your father deprived your mother's relatives of all his property at his death."

"So?"

"Your father's property remains here," Chosadziwa interpreted. "It doesn't go back to your mother's relatives as it would have done if he'd lived there."

"We always knew you were intelligent," Madala commented, "even though a slave."

"That's a sharp one," echoed Mdoda, eyeing the youth speculatively.

"What happens to the children, then?" Chosadziwa asked.

The question gathered weight in the following silence. There were a few squirms and coughs. Someone opened a snuff box, sniffed, and sneezed violently.

"This is where the thorn hurts most for the children," Madala said slowly.

"How?" Dzunzo could not understand why the elders should skirt around the main point like inexperienced swimmers avoiding a deep pool.

"They can choose to remain in their father's village or go back to join the relatives in their mother's village."

"But he has relatives here." Chosadziwa could not contain himself. He was way ahead of Dzunzo.

"We trace our blood through our mother's line." Madala shook his head. "That's why we build in the woman's village."

"You mean now it's up to me to choose to stay here or go back to my mother's home?"

"We knew you would see the point."

"But I was born here," Dzunzo protested. "This is my home. I don't know any other relatives."

"We have told you the alternatives." Madala was pensive. "Some of your father's relatives are here. They would like to know what your decision is going to be."

Dzunzo looked around the gloom. Most of the faces were indistinguishable. "Is Uncle Mponda here?"

"He went to the lake yesterday for a month of fishing. You know how he loves his fish."

"Is Chimwala here?"

"He's gone elephant hunting again."

"What about Grandmother Nadzonzi?"

"She's too old and sick to be part of this."

"Aunt Makoko?"

"That half-crazy widow?"

"Did any of my father's relatives know you were coming to tell me about this *chitengwa* thing tonight?" There was a lump in his throat.

"They know the customs of our people. They are old enough."

"What did they think about it?" He shivered uncontrollably. He had just realised why his closest relatives were not amongst the elders that night.

"They are not here to tell us."

Dzunzo turned to the anonymous faces around him. Chosadziwa looked expectantly at him. Dzunzo felt helpless, like a mouse in a spiked bamboo trap. Every turn he took hurt him. He remembered his mother's

12

words: "You'll remember me when I die, my son." He swallowed the lump in his throat and looked round again. He noticed that no one wanted to look him in the eye. Mdoda thumped his snuff box again and took out a pinch.

"It is also the custom of our people," said Madala after a long pause, to burn the house of the deceased a few days after the burial, to avoid misfortune from the ancestral spirits. It's all part of the final funeral rites."

There was a loud sneeze from Mdoda. Dzunzo jumped up with a whimper. He did not know whether it was a reaction to the loud noise or the explosiveness of the news. He sat down again, opening and shutting his mouth wordlessly like a frog. His head was whirling.

"But ... but ...," he mumbled in the dark, "if you burn the house, where am I going to live?"

"Exactly," said Madala pensively. "That's why we came to warn you in good time, so you can decide what to do."

"When is the house-burning ceremony?" Dzunzo felt as if there was an enormous dam in his throat threatening to burst him wide open.

"There's plenty of time: next week."

"Who does the burning?"

"All the elders. It's purely routine."

The elders left Dzunzo in no doubt as to the finality of the villagers' decision. He did not think he wanted to witness the fire ceremony.

Chapter Two

Crossing the River

"What is there to go back to?" Dzunzo had asked pointedly. It was this question that decided both of them to go on with the journey, omens or no omens. They watched the chameleon on his agonisingly slow walk across the path. The reptile had taken on the dirty brown colour of the path. Chosadziwa burst into the chameleon's song to accompany its progress:

> *Chameleon, why are your eyes swollen?*
> *There's death at home.*
> *Do not laugh, children.*
> *It's empty, empty, empty.*

A front pincer leg opened, stretched, hovered, and tentatively placed itself forward. One bulging eye swivelled round to look at the boys, the other scanned the terrain ahead. A hind leg detached itself and followed the front one.

> *I shall leave this village.*
> *You stay behind and build this village.*
> *Look at my homestead.*
> *It's empty, empty, empty.*

Mottled green replaced brown as it approached the shrubs and grasses. It Was almost totally green as it disappeared into the undergrowth.

"Now we can go on," Chosadziwa ended his song and concluded, "although I still feel it's not safe. We'll meet with misfortune along the way."

"Let's go on." Dzunzo's mind went back yet again to the hopeless situation they had left in Maitsalani, his father's village. Once the boys had told them of their decision, the elders had been very helpful, if not actually enthusiastic, about giving them directions.

"I remember going to Mwanalilenji, Naliyela's village, once ..." Madala said.

"I was the male *nkhoswe* on Ndasauka's side," Mdoda reminisced. "The negotiations took several weeks and involved more than one trip from here."

Before the house-burning ceremony, the boys knew how to get to Mwanalilenji. They also knew how long, very long, it would take to get there. Even the elders had taken a long time on their trips.

It was Chosadziwa's foresight that had made the boys prepare *kamba,* provisions for the long journey.

"I know this is the rainy season," Chosadziwa had said. "We'll find plenty of wild fruit or small animals to eat on the way. But it's better to prepare our own food to take." He had prepared *chiwamba* of various kinds, including birds. He had also prepared *chikande* and *mkate,* two different kinds of bread, made from tubers and bananas respectively.

"Don't worry about *thobwa* for a drink," Chosadziwa joked. "It'll just burden us. We'll have lots of *mateme,* and maybe coconuts by the riverside."

It must have been the time he had spent in the hills and forests with the elephant hunters that had made Chosadziwa so knowledgeable about survival on a long trip. Here they were living on dried meat, dried sauce, dried cake, and other chewables tied up in little bundles. They supplemented the home-cooked foods with *mpoza, nthudza,* and *masau* they picked from the trees on the way. There was no cause for thirst, either. It had rained steadily the first few days, making their progress slow as they took refuge under thick foliage or overhanging rocks on the hillsides.

"Use this stick." Chosadziwa gave Dzunzo a branch he had broken off from a tree. He showed him how to beat the accumulated rainwater off the shrubs and grasses by the wayside before they passed. The sodden blades and leaves, leaning heavily over the path, would otherwise have drenched their clothes and bodies, hindering their progress as if it was still raining. Dzunzo followed Chosadziwa's example and beat his way up and down, along the slippery path.

15

No one had wept as the boys had gone round to the uncles, aunts, and grandparents. Even their playmates, who were really Dzunzo's cousins, had hidden their embarrassment behind solemn faces. No one had escorted them to the edge of the village, or the river, or the forest, to see them off. It had been a gloomy, cheerless start, and the boys' hearts had been heavy with suppressed emotions.

"You have decided wisely," some of the elders had commented. "It is good to be with your own people."

"When you grow old," others had pointed out, "you'll appreciate the customs of our people. In any case, it is better to die among your own relatives."

"Remember me to your uncle, Mlauzi," had been Mdoda's parting shot. "Remind him of old Mdoda who nearly married his other sister when I went for the *unkhoswe.*"

"We are young," one of Dzunzo's cousins had said. "We are sure to meet again before we die."

At dawn the next day, the boys had taken the big path that led out of the village to the foothills. The house was to be burned later that morning. Dzunzo had reviewed the property his father had left behind: how much he could have taken if they had allowed him. Between Chosadziwa and himself, on foot, they could only carry so much. As it turned out, they carried only the food they needed for the trip.

"Let them keep everything," had been Dzunzo's angry decision in the end. "They have more or less confiscated my father's property anyway."

"We could herd some of the animals in front of us as we go."

"Do you think my relatives will allow us to do that?"

True enough, animals and poultry had disappeared under their very noses.

"We don't burn these along with the house." A whole pen had been emptied to fill his uncle's.

"These always go to the chief." A kraal had been impounded.

"It's a pity you can't take this furniture with you." The movable pieces had been carted away.

By the time the boys had been leaving, they had literally been left only with the clothes on their backs. Dzunzo's cousins had had a share in the distribution of the widower's son's property. "These don't fit you any more, do they?" or "These are now rags. You don't want to burden yourself with them on such a long journey." or "Your Uncle Mlauzi will fit you out with new clothes." It had gone on and on like that, as if Dzunzo too had died, and his clothes could be left to the living. Chosadziwa, who had been roasting grain and preparing the *kamba,* was left only with his old working clothes. He looked a sight on the trip, especially when their clothes got soaked. Chosadziwa, of all people, had not been in a position to protest when his clothes had been impounded. He was only a slave.

"The elders said your mother left Mwanalilenji a long time ago." Chosadziwa broke into Dzunzo's reverie. "Do you know if she ever went back there for a visit?"

"She didn't tell me."

"Has anyone from her village ever visited her at Maitsalani?"

"No. Why?"

"She didn't even go back to her relatives to introduce you?"

"Not that I remember."

"So her relatives at Mwanalilenji have never seen you?"

"I don't think so."

"So when we get there, no one will even recognise you?"

"How can they, if they've never set eyes on me before?"

"So how will they know you?"

"We'll go by what the elders told us."

"That's not enough. How will you prove that you're your mother's son?"

"There's only one Ndasauka, my father, who took Naliyela, my

17

mother, from Mwanalilenji Village. Everyone will know who I am, when I tell them my background."

Chosadziwa was silent. They continued beating their way up the path.

"There seems to have been more rain where we're going," Chosadziwa commented, a few paces ahead of Dzunzo.

It was true. The path was a rivulet now, with water streaming down the hillside to the plains. The boys' general direction was towards the plains, where Mwanalilenji lay.

"With all these rains, some rivers must be in flood."

"I hope not."

"Why?"

"I can't swim. I'm a hillside dweller."

"I can. I've even swum in the big lake."

It was pointless now to use their sticks to beat the water off the bushes. With luck, their sodden clothes would dry before they reached their destination. In spite of the rain, or perhaps because of it, the trees around them were alive with birds, insects and other life. A pigeon crooned mournfully to their left.

"Remember that one?" Chosadziwa asked.

"It's a pigeon."

"Do you remember the song that goes with it?"

"It reminds me of my mother."

"How does it go?"

Dzunzo sang it more to relieve the monotony of the journey than to please Chosadziwa:

> *When mother died*
> *In a mouse trap,*
> *She cried uuh!*
> *Uuh! Uuh! Uuh!*

"You know it, then."

"Of course, I do," Dzunzo said indignantly. Chosadziwa just laughed and carried on walking. Dzunzo sometimes found his companion irritating, especially when he showed off his skills or talents. It was as if he himself was just an ignorant nobody.

"We're coming to Mzimundilinde," Chosadziwa announced just ahead of him.

The elders had told them that Mzimundilinde was their first landmark for Mwanalilenji. Indeed, the vegetation had changed. The boys caught sight of Mwanalilenji plain between the *mpinjipinji* and sausage trees. Dzunzo recognised some of the hollow grasses from which they used to make flutes. These gave way to *nsenjere* grass and reeds. In fact, they had heard the roar of the river long before Chosadziwa announced it. The rivulets had become larger and more numerous. The soil sank under their bare feet. They trudged on, sliding in the mud.

"Hold on to the branches," Chosadziwa advised. "Avoid the grasses."

"Why?"

"The blades can cut your palms."

Dzunzo frequently regretted asking foolish questions which he could have answered himself. He thought it was because Chosadziwa had made him depend on him for most things. Sometimes, he found himself deliberately not thinking so Chosadziwa would take over. He took Chosadziwa's advice too late. An involuntary cry escaped his lips.

"What happened?"

"I cut myself."

"I told you to watch out!" Chosadziwa stopped to look at Dzunzo's bleeding hand. The red dripped into the rivulet and dissolved in the mud. Chosadziwa looked round him wildly and then ran into the.bush to his right. He came back with *chitimbe* leaves. He was chewing some. He took Dzunzo's limp hand and spat the *chitimbe* poultice onto the wound, chanting, *"Little wound, heal! Little wound, heal!"*

The bleeding slowed down. Chosadziwa continued his chant. The skin closed up. The bleeding stopped.

"What happened?" Dzunzo was amazed.

"It's a magic formula the elephant hunters taught me," Chosadziwa boasted. "I can heal any wound with it."

"It's the leaves," Dzunzo corrected.

"Of course, with the leaves too."

They went on. Dzunzo reflected that there had been more blood than pain. It was amazing, all the same, how Chosadziwa had healed him. In a day or two, he would not even notice a scar.

The roar of the river turned to thunder. The two boys could hardly hear each other's voices now.

"I told you."

"What?"

"We're unlucky."

"Look!"

They stepped forward to see a mass of water frothing and bubbling over huge boulders. Dzunzo's heart sank. The boys looked high and low.

"There's no tree bridge." It was an unnecessary observation. Apart from some broken trunks and branches stuck between the boulders, there was nothing suitable for crossing Mzimundilinde.

"It's death to be caught in that torrent." Again, it was obvious. Apart from the flotsam and jetsam, the jagged edges of the rocks and trunks could really cause serious injuries.

"Let's try further downstream," Chosadziwa finally said.

The boys clung to creepers, vines and branches as they slithered in mud, over rocks and fallen trees on the banks.

"Surely your relatives must have a place they use to cross the river so as to get to the hills or visit their neighbours."

"I don't know," Dzunzo said breathlessly as he slipped in the mud.

"Those rocks look like a possibility."

They both gazed at some rocks that looked as if they had been arranged deliberately across the river. Some were almost completely submerged, some showed the tips, but of others more was showing.

"Wait!" Chosadziwa looked speculatively at the rocks, then at Dzunzo. "Give me your clothes!"

"Why'?" Dzunzo was surprised.

"You can't swim." Chosadziwa was taking off his clothes. "If you fall in, your clothes will get wet."

"They're already wet."

"Only the shorts. Your shirt is still reasonably dry. You don't want them to get any wetter than they are."

Dzunzo complied. Chosadziwa rolled Dzunzo's and his own clothes into a bundle, tied them with a creeper, and strapped them to his head.

"I'll go first. Just do as I do. Hold onto this stick. If either of us falls into the water, the other will pull him out."

They jumped onto the nearest rock. Chosadziwa felt ahead of him with another stick to identify a submerged rock, Dzunzo followed, holding onto the other end of the guiding stick. The two negotiated the entire width of the river in this fashion. When they got to the other side without any major difficulty, Dzunzo breathed a sigh of relief.

Chapter Three

The Slave

"These clothes certainly fit me." Chosadziwa had put on Dzunzo's clothes. He pranced up and down, admiring himself.

"Of course," Dzunzo agreed. "You're only a year or two older than me. Besides, you're slim, so you look younger than your age. The way we have grown up together, we're almost brothers."

"We ARE brothers. Remember the oath?"

Dzunzo remembered the exchange of blood. The two boys had been out in the forest collecting *nthudza* fruit. In the course of sorting the ripe from the unripe ones, a thorn from the tree had scratched Dzunzo's arm, drawing a little blood.

"Let's mix our blood," Chosadziwa had piped up.

"What do you mean?"

Chosadziwa had bent the branch of the *nthudza* tree and pricked himself with a thorn. He had held his arm next to Dzunzo's, and rubbed the pricks to mix the blood. "With this mixing of blood," he had intoned, "we are now blood brothers."

"We've always been brothers."

"I know," Chosadziwa had laughed. "But now we're in each other's blood. Inseparable."

"I see what you mean. People have always thought we're brothers, anyway."

"Your father took me as his second son. He never treated me as a slave."

"Yes, he loved you as much as he loved me. We're almost twins."

Dzunzo looked at Chosadziwa again, speculatively, and nodded.

"Let's see if your mother's people will treat us as such." A gleam came into Chosadziwa's eyes.

"What do you mean?"

"We'll play a game of twin brothers."

"I don't understand." Dzunzo did not like the tone that had crept into Chosadziwa's voice. It did not sound like him anymore.

"I'll keep your clothes on. You'll wear mine. Let's see if they recognise who their true nephew is."

"You think they won't know?"

"If they haven't seen you since you were born, how will they tell us apart?"

"That's true."

"Well then, let's see if they're clever enough to see through our game."

"I don't think that's wise." Dzunzo shivered a little.

"Come on, it's only a game, just for fun."

"All right." Dzunzo was reluctant. Something told him, as he put on Chosadziwa's rags, that it was not right, especially on their first visit to his mother's village. However, Chosadziwa had always been full of such pranks. Some of them had been fun, but others had not worked out the way they had been intended. For such, there had been so much to make amends for afterwards.

The boys continued their journey. The path grew wider and smoother after the river. They passed an anthill with a whole tree growing right through it. A bird whistled in the foliage above them. It paused in its song.

"That's the *mw iyo,*" Chosadziwa interpreted.

"What does it do?"

"It's an ominous bird, depending..

"Depending on what?"

"Wait!" Chosadziwa stood listening intently. "Don't interrupt until we finish. I'll follow its song."

The shrike resumed its whistling up in the branches. They could not see it. The branches and leaves of the ant tree were so thick. Chosadziwa chanted after it.

> *Mwiyo! Mwiyo!*
> *Where we're going*
> *They'll give us rice*
> *With lots of meat!*
> *When I stay quiet*
> *You stop whistling too!*

The bird song ceased.

"We're in luck!" Chosadziwa jumped up excitedly. "They'll prepare a feast for us!"

"Just because of the bird?"

"If the bird had continued whistling when I ordered it to stop, we would have got a miserable welcome. But since it stopped immediately, we can expect at least a big meal."

Dzunzo had always marvelled at Chosadziwa's vast knowledge of the world around them. How could such a small boy, captured in the forest, have acquired such wisdom. Who had taught him all these things? The elephant hunters? His parents? Was he an ordinary child or not? Dzunzo thought hard.

"If the *mwiyo* bird is ominous," Dzunzo broke the silence after a while as they walked on, "We must be nearing Mwanalilenji."

"It won't be far now. We should be there before sunset."

"Then," Dzunzo started tentatively, "I think we should get back into our own clothes."

"I thought we had agreed to play a game of make-believe?"

"I don't think we should play such games on grown-ups we don't know. My Uncle Mlauzi and Aunt Nalichowa must be old now, maybe older than my parents. They won't like such childish games."

"Let's see what happens. As soon as we know they can't tell who their nephew is, we'll reveal ourselves."

"You promise?"

"It's a promise. We're brothers, remember?"

Still Dzunzo was perturbed. What if the game backfired? The boys were complete strangers in Mwanalilenji. How could they play such a game and hope the others would be amused?

The forest trees were thinning now, and being replaced by shrubs and grasses.

"This must have been a garden in the past," Chosadziwa hazarded. "How do you know?"

"These shrubs haven't grown back into trees." Chosadziwa was looking about him. "Your people must be rice-growers."

"I don't see any rice around."

"If you look closely, you'll notice that there is a lot of *gugu* and *sichilile* grass mixed with the *kamphe* grass."

"So what has that got to do with rice?"

"Where *gugu* and *sichilile* grow, rice grows too, abundantly. You can see the tufts at the tips like rice grain. In fact, during a famine, people eat *gugu* and *sichilile* as rice. Some people can't tell the difference between faya rice and these grasses, once cooked."

"But you can?"

Chosadziwa chuckled, pulled out one of the grasses in question, and started chewing it, after breaking open the husk. There was a strong smell of rice cooking, too.

"Let's run for our lives." Chosadziwa matched his words with action.

"Why?" Dzunzo dashed after the receding figure.

"There are witches there, cooking rice."

"How can you tell?"

"When you smell rice in the woods or grasses, the witches are cooking it. They're invisible, but they're preparing their midday meal. It wasn't our rice you smelled out there. Ours has yet to be cooked, after the *alendo siyawo* bird has sighted us."

"You mean another bird will announce our coming?"

"For visitors from far away, yes," Chosadziwa explained impatiently. "Everything is related — people, trees, birds, animals, reptiles ..."

"But how?"

"Wait and see. Stranger things have yet to come."

Chosadziwa slowed down to a trot. Dzunzo did the same. Soon they were back to the fast lope of travellers on the road.

"These clothes are really comfortable." Chosadziwa stretched himself and pranced about on the pathway. "It's nice to feel the clothes of a freeborn."

"My father clothed you well, too."

"Yes, discarded clothes from you. I've never enjoyed the feel of new clothes on my skin."

"But sometimes I gave you my new clothes to wear."

"They were still hand-me-downs. They weren't bought or made for me. I only tasted the new clothes meant for you, not directly. That's the difference."

"Still, my father treated you like his own child."

"I know, but once a slave, always a slave. Do you know what it is like to be a slave, you?"

"I was almost like one in my father's village back there. After his death, I didn't feel at home anymore."

"Don't confuse being an orphan with being a slave."

"But my parents are dead now, the same as yours."

"We're not the same. You were freeborn all your life. When your parents died, your relatives sent you back to your mother's village. I have no parents and no relatives to go back to. You're going to Mwanalilenji as a freeborn. I'm going with you as your slave, not a freeborn."

"But now that we're going to Mwanalilenji, where no one knows us, no one need know that you're my slave. We'll go to my uncle Mlauzi and aunt Nalichowa as brothers — which is true — our blood mingled."

"In my heart, I'll always know, and in yours, you'll always remember, that I was and still am a slave boy."

"But my father's death freed you. He was your master, and now you're free."

"He bought me, he was my master, and he alone can free me. His instructions were for me to serve you. I'm still doing it, even though you're my age mate and companion."

"Let's start afresh." Dzunzo stopped Chosadziwa. He walked round to stand in front of him, and placed earnest hands on both shoulders. "As my father's only son, I'm setting you free. There now — you're free."

"You mean I can leave you and go wherever I want?" Chosadziwa spread his arms out.

"Yes."

"Seriously?"

"Absolutely."

"But where do I go to? I can't remember where I came from. As a matter of fact, with the kind of freedom your father gave me, I could have escaped a hundred times before this. But I couldn't. Much as I know the wilds, I cannot retrace the steps those elephant hunters took. They hunted here, there and everywhere, for months on end. We wandered in the forests, over the hills, down in the valleys, roasting elephant meat, hunting buffalo, selling in this village, bartering in that, till I lost all sense of direction. Now I simply can't go back home, even if I wanted to."

27

"Then come with me as a freeborn. You were never really a slave. Those people kidnapped you. They did not buy you. Your parents were still alive. They did not sell you."

"Your father bought me from those hunters for bags of sorghum. Even if I'd still been a freeborn under the hunters, your father's buying me turned me into a slave."

"It's only you who chooses to think so. With me, you're free, you're my brother. Where we're going I will introduce you as such. They don't know how many children my parents had, therefore it'll be easy to tell them we're brothers. Only one or two years separate us, in fact, so it's not a lie to say you're my elder brother: the first and second born. Can't you see it?"

"I hadn't thought about it like that before. Let me work it out."

They walked past the abandoned fields in silence for a while. Chosadziwa broke the silence again as they moved into what seemed to be the last lap of their journey.

"About your relatives," Chosadziwa began. "Even if your mother and her relatives did not visit each other, what about when she died? Didn't they come to the funeral?"

Dzunzo thought back to his mother's illness, then her death. His mind scanned the faces of the mourners gathered at his father's house, and later at the graveyard. They were all from Maitsalani Village and neighbouring ones. These were the familiar faces of those who frequented the village, whether or not there was a funeral. The *adzukulu,* too, the funeral friends, were also from the next village. The women helping in the wailing, the men digging the grave and refilling it afterwards were from the same nearby villages. The men and women who stayed on for several days afterwards to sleep at the house of the bereaved were also familiar faces. Dzunzo's tear-blurred eyes had noticed all these facts.

"No," he mumbled at last. "None came from Mwanalilenji."

"That's strange," Chosadziwa murmured. "Even if they missed your outdooring ceremony, they should have christened you — that's an important ceremony in any family's life. It's a big ceremony for the first

28

child. And to think that they didn't even attend your mother's funeral! It's as if they had entirely cut her off from their list of kin."

"Maybe they heard late about her death."

"A message would have been sent. If they couldn't attend the actual burial, they should have come to the *sadaka,* the commemoration of the dead."

"My father would have told me," Dzunzo said vehemently. "It would have been the time to introduce me to them."

"Are you sure?"

"Why should he have hidden them from me? I'm the only son of Naliyela. The relatives from Mwanalilenji would have asked to meet any children. But nothing of the sort happened."

"So they really don't know their daughter's son, when he comes home to stay?" Chosadziwa asked pointedly.

"I told you, no one knows me. No one has seen me. They don't even know my name."

Chosadziwa walked on in a turmoil of silence. Here were possibilities he had never imagined before. Of course, at Maitsalani he would not have thought of escaping. It was true he had no recollection of how to get back to his own village. He had now been freed by his little master, but still could not leave. He could not go back home. Perhaps there was no need to go back. Why should he? Why shouldn't he go with his blood brother and continue enjoying the same kind of freedom and companionship he had enjoyed before? As Dzunzo had pointed out, no one in Mwanalilenji need ever know the truth. Why not play Dzunzo's twist in the game to the full?

It wouldn't be a game anymore, come to think of it. Chosadziwa himself had started it a long time ago, with the mixing of blood. At Mzimundilinde River, it had continued with the exchange of clothes. He was still wearing Dzunzo's clothes. Why not play the game more seriously and introduce himself as the true son of Naliyela? Why not? Dzunzo had suggested that already. Yes, but Dzunzo need not, should not be there. Sooner or later,

Dzunzo would reveal by his actions or even speech who the true son was. How could he silence Dzunzo?

They were passing by the Mwanalilenji graveyard. Chosadziwa recognised the grave trees: *nkhadzi, mlombwa, thundu,* and even *mvunguti.* It was a big graveyard, which meant it was an ancient village, too, with so many generations of dead. Why not get rid of Dzunzo and throw him in the graveyard? He would be with his ancestors then. They would surely welcome their young son into the other world. No, his body would be discovered, even if he buried him elsewhere. They were too near the village now. Questions would be asked, coincidences puzzled over, and Chosadziwa would be exposed as the perpetrator.

What about going on with the game but making sure that Dzunzo did not talk? What if ...? Chosadziwa's mind reeled. He heard the *alendo siyawo* bird.

"Ah!" Chosadziwa started excitedly, "that's the bird song I was waiting for."

"What bird song?"

"Listen to what it says." Chosadziwa took the same stance as he had done for the shrike. He interpreted for Dzunzo. "Here come the visitors! *Alendo siyawo!* Here come the visitors!"

"We're home at last!" Dzunzo shouted.

"Wait!" Chosadziwa ordered. "There's one last ritual you don't know about that we must perform before entering the village."

"What is it?" Dzunzo was impatient.

"Just do as I say." Chosadziwa went to one of the mounds under a *thundu* tree. He bent and scooped up a handful of earth.

"What are you doing?" Dzunzo was apprehensive.

"*Thundu* is for the great men who have died. They're buried under it. Come!"

Dzunzo was powerless. Chosadziwa's manner was changed. His voice took on the same chanting tone he had adopted earlier.

"By your ancestor's dust I sprinkle over your head and mouth," Chosadziwa intoned, "you will be able to see and hear, but will not utter a word. As they are dumb below, so will you be dumb!"

"Th—th—bb—gg—" Dzunzo uttered sounds, but no word came out of his mouth.

"It works!" Chosadziwa said gleefully. "Now we will go into your village with you as my slave boy and me the freeborn!"

Dzunzo followed Chosadziwa mutely. The *alendo siyawo* crooned an accompaniment to their entry into Mwanalilenji: *"Look, here are the strangers!"*

Chapter Four

The Homecoming

Mwanalilenji — "what can a child cry for?" — was so named because it was completely self-sustaining. Everything the people needed could be found in the fields, rivers, forests and hills around them. The village traced its history back to Kaphirintiwa, humankind's birthplace. Ancient belief had it that when Mbona, their guardian spirit, had fled from Msinja to found his own shrine in Nsanje, he had sojourned there. In return for Mwanalilenji's hospitality, Mbona had given the people faya rice. The people were proud of this strain, one that could not grow anywhere else. It withstood the onslaughts of *nadanga* and other weeds. It tillered quickly. It could survive and ripen even after scanty rains. Regardless of what time of year it was sown, it would still ripen and produce a good harvest. It yielded the long narrow golden grain that every farmer wanted to see in his *nkhokwe* granary and on his plate. The best seeds were selected and stored separately for planting the following rainy season.

Mwanalilenji spread along both sides of Mzimundilinde River. Between the banks and the village were *dimba* and rice fields. Rice and sorghum were the people's staple foods. The other source of food was the birds that came to feed on the rice. Hundreds and hundreds of them descended on the grain when it started to ripen at the end of the rainy season. This was also the time to harvest. Mlauzi and Nalichowa were seated near the rice store by the side of the main house. Mlauzi's close-cropped hair was streaked with grey, as was his wife's. Both were old enough to have grandchildren.

Thump! Thump! Mlauzi was beating the rice drying on the reed mats with a stick to separate the grain from the stems. The grain broke loose and fell between the other stems to accumulate on the mat. Nalichowa collected it into a heap on another mat. From this heap, she scooped some rice and winnowed it in the flat open winnowing basket. There was another heap of winnowed rice beside her, free of leaves, stems and other debris.

Husband and wife were, in fact, surrounded by mats of rice, with the granary behind them. Mlauzi was actually sitting on the low platform protruding from the granary. To reach the rice on the mat, he had to lean low over his bent knees. Nalichowa was sitting in the characteristic female pose: both legs bent at the knees to one side. This left space for the arms to go up and down, to and fro, churning to allow the grain to rise to the top of the winnowing basket. Nalichowa's left eyelid twitched.

"We're going to have visitors," she mused silently. When the eyelid twitched again, more rapidly this time, she repeated herself aloud.

"What ... What?" Mlauzi was startled. They had not exchanged any words for some time, each one busy with the work at hand and his or her own thoughts. The noises around them included the *phwiti* birds hopping and twittering at the far end of the mats.

Nalichowa picked up some blighted grain from the basket and threw it aside. She repeated what she had said, giving her reasons. "

Are you expecting anybody?"

"Not really," she laughed, then stopped abruptly. "Listen." *"Alendo siyawo! "* the bird announced. *"Look, there are the visitors!"*

"The bird confirms my predictions."

"There you go again!" Mlauzi continued his thump! thump!

"My eyelid never goes wrong."

Their grandchildren were eating *mgodo,* uncooked rice mash, on the *khonde* at the front of the house. Their eating was punctuated by angry exchanges and cries from the younger ones, whose hands were slapped away from the plate of mash. Repeated reprimands from Nalichowa had not resolved the quarrels. In the end, she just left them to sort themselves out. The older sons were out in the fields chasing the birds from the rice. The older daughters had gone to draw water for the evening.

"Look," the bird insisted, *"there are the visitors!"*

"We haven't had any visitors for a long time now."

"My eyelid hasn't twitched for a long time, either. These must be visitors from far away."

"This is the harvest season. Everyone is busy with their own crops. Who'd go visiting at this time?"

"I'd better put some rice on the fire."

"How do you know they're our visitors?"

"There's the *mwichire* bird on the roof now." Nalichowa pointed to a bird with red plumage. It opened its throat.

"*Leave out some food!*" it chirped. "*Mwichire kamba! Give the strangers some food!*"

"This is too much." Mlauzi straightened up. The bird didn't stop delivering its message.

"*Alendo! Alendo!*" chanted their grandchildren from the *khonde*. "*Visitors! Visitors!*"

"You see what I mean?"

Mlauzi leaned sideways to look up the path that led to the house. He saw the figures of two tired looking boys.

"They're just boys," he dismissed them and went on threshing.

"They aren't ours."

"They could be anybody's."

"But they're not from Mwanalilenji." Nalichowa's gaze was unfaltering." Look at their clothes."

"They seem to be heading for this house, too," agreed Mlauzi, peering at the two figures.

"Of course, they're following the *mwichire* bird."

"Is this the house of Uncle Mlauzi?" they heard one of the boys ask.

"Yees!" chorused the children on the *khonde*.

"And Aunt Nalichowa?"

34

The chorus was repeated.

"They seem to know us." Nalichowa stated the obvious.

"Go and find out who they are," Mlauzi ordered imperiously.

Nalichowa straightened up. She dusted herself as she walked round to the front. She found the boys already sitting on the *khonde.*

"So it's our visitors!" she said unnecesssarily, as she shook the hands of each boy.

"Yes, Aunt Nalichowa," answered Chosadziwa.

"Ng—Ph—Th—" muttered Dzunzo, vigorously shaking his head.

"Your brother doesn't speak?" Nalichowa marvelled at Dzunzo.

"He's just my slave," Chosadziwa said dismissively. "He's mute."

"Th—Ph—Ng—." Dzunzo got up agitatedly. Chosadziwa stood up, too.

"What's he doing?" Nalichowa shifted her stance.

"He sometimes gets too excited," Chosadziwa explained. "Sit down, Dzunzo. We're home at last. Here's my Aunt."

"Is he all right?" Nalichowa looked closely at Dzunzo.

"He'll be all right soon." Chosadziwa held him down.

"Who are you?" Nalichowa asked.

"I'm Chosadziwa, the son of Naliyela ..."

Dzunzo shook his head, beat his chest, and angry tears started rolling down his cheeks. Chosadziwa held onto him even more tightly.

"This is Dzunzo," Chosadziwa went on. "Ndasauka, my father, gave him to me when I was young. We grew up together. So I brought him along when father died."

"You're Ndasauka's son?"

"Yes."

"Where is Naliyela?"

"She died, too!"

Nalichowa started wailing, "My sister-in-law! My brother!"

"What is it?" Mlauzi strode up.

"There's your nephew!" She pointed to Chosadziwa.

"Uncle Mlauzi." Chosadziwa stood up. "I'm Chosadziwa, your sister Naliyela's son."

"Ph—Th—Ng—"

"What's happening here?" Mlauzi looked at Dzunzo struggling in Chosadziwa's grip.

"He's mute. Sometimes he has epileptic fits. That's why I have to hold him down. He can hurt himself."

"Will you stop wailing, woman?" Mlauzi shouted at his wife. "I can't hear what he's saying."

"People do come back from the grave!" Nalichowa cried as she went to the back of the house to wail with more freedom.

"Now," Mlauzi sat down near the boys, "start from the beginning."

"My mother, your sister," Chosadziwa began, "died a long time ago."

"Why didn't they tell us?"

"I don't know, uncle. Your brother-in-law died last month."

"Did he? Why didn't any messages reach us? Is that why you're here?"

"No ... Yes ... This is the sad part." Chosadziwa's face fell.

"What's sadder than the news of your parents' death?"

"The elders, my other relatives at Maitsalani, didn't want us. They told us to come here. They said this is where I belong."

"Of course, you belong here. Who is this mute here?"

"He's my slave boy. Father bought him from some elephant hunters."

"Ph—Th—Ng—." Dzunzo struggled harder.

"Is he always like this?"

"Sometimes I have to tie him up. He rolls on the ground or beats his head against walls or trees as he tries to speak."

"Did Ndasauka buy him like this?"

"Yes, but he was calmer then. It's only after father's death that he started getting violent. I had problems getting here alone with him." "You must be tired and hungry."

"Tired, yes, but we had lots of fruit on the way."

"Fruit doesn't last long in the stomach. Your aunt was preparing some rice. Bengo! Limbani!" Mlauzi called to the young boys. "Catch that cock. My nephew will have a feast tonight."

The boys who had been called started chasing a medium-sized rooster which, as soon as it realised their intention, broke into a run. The boys gleefully ran after it. They knew the head, the drumsticks and the intestines were theirs for roasting as payment for their labour.

"We'll have to tie your slave up. He's going to hurt you. Lunza! Bring some rope here!"

"Aah!" Dzunzo roared. "Ph—Th—Ng—." He struggled spiritedly as Mlauzi and Chosadziwa between them tied up his legs and arms. He lay panting and making animal noises on the ground. By this time, some of the neighbours had come over to Mlauzi's house.

"What is it?" they asked. "What's happening here? Why the crying?"

It was Mlauzi's turn to explain.

"This," he hugged Chosadziwa, "is my nephew, Naliyela's son. The *mtengwa* who went to live in Maitsalani, beyond the hills. Let him tell us his story in full himself."

Dzunzo squirmed. Someone put rags in his mouth to shut him up. In his supine, mute state, Dzunzo heard Chosadziwa's story as he would have narrated it himself. Chosadziwa just doctored the facts. placing himself as the true son of Ndasauka and Naliyela. while Dzunzo was the slave.

"But how did you know about us?"

37

"Madala and Mdoda, two of the elders, still remember you. They gave us directions," Chosadziwa said easily. "But my mother told me about you and Mwanalilenji a long time before that."

"Even our names?"

"That's why I asked for you by name when we got here."

Mlauzi looked at the other listeners significantly. It was as if he wanted them to endorse the story too. Nalichowa, who had rejoined them when Chosadziwa was giving his account, started sobbing again.

"Give the boy some hot water to have a bath," Mlauzi instructed her.

"The water is already in the shed."

"My nephew," Mlauzi hugged Chosadziwa again, "go and freshen up after your long journey. Tomorrow, you'll join your cousins at the riverside. Apasani's clothes should just about fit you. Dumbo will show you the way."

Chosadziwa let himself be led behind the house. Dzunzo rolled to and fro on the ground, groaning.

"What does a man do in this case?" Mlauzi looked at his neighbours again.

"A great wrong has been done," one said.

"They shouldn't have chased the boy away," another added.

"We're to blame." Mlauzi shook his head. "When Ndasauka took my sister away, we did not follow her. After she left, we just gave her up for dead. She never visited us and we in turn never visited her."

"At least they gave you back her son," came a woman's voice from the far end of the khonde .

"Yes," agreed the first neighbour, "although it was cruel to send him away like that."

"What about the property?" Mlauzi queried.

"You heard what your nephew said. How each relative grabbed whatever they could, even before the two boys had left Maitsalani."

38

"Yes, I suppose I should be content with having my nephew back, and even this slave boy."

"What are you going to do with him?"

"Send him to the fields along with the others. We can't feed him if he doesn't work."

Dzunzo knew that he would have to comply with what Mlauzi said. He was tired, hungry and angry. However, no amount of gnashing his teeth, hitting his head against the ground or roaring would help him. His worst punishment was to be struck dumb. He could not speak of the great crime that Chosadziwa had committed against him, his father and his people. He blamed himself for the trick that Chosadziwa had played. Dzunzo himself had naively told the slave all the family facts and secrets.

Chosadziwa, bathing in the shed, congratulated himself on a fine piece of work. For as long as Dzunzo remained dumb, he was safe. He did not know how long the spell would last, if it would at all. All he knew was that it had worked on Dzunzo. He now had to pray that it would not be broken. Till then he would enjoy rice and chicken. He looked forward to meeting his new cousins.

Chapter Five

The First Night

Mlauzi and Nalichowa did not allow Chosadziwa to go to the *gowero,* the boys' sleeping place, immediately after the chicken and rice. Mlauzi made the boy go over again the story of his travels, then life in Maitsalani. Dzunzo had been given a separate meal of *therere* and sorghum porridge. After his efforts to free himself and to reveal the truth, he was subdued throughout. Since he, too, was going to sleep with the boys, he was forced to hear again the story Chosadziwa had cooked up about his childhood and life in Maitsalani. The couple only released Chosadziwa reluctantly when they were tired. Dzunzo was referred to as the "slave" throughout. No one used his proper name. He sat wretched, away from his cousins and the storyteller.

"Sleep well, my nephew and children," Mlauzi bade them all goodnight. "Tomorrow, we'll go to the fields together. As you saw for yourself, this is harvest time. We shall need your help."

"Of course." Chosadziwa got up to join Apasani and his brothers. "And this slave here. He's a hard worker."

"He'd better be. He has to earn his keep."

The *gowero* was four houses away from Mlauzi's. About a dozen boys slept with Apasani, including his brothers and close cousins. Apasani's *gowero,* as it was called, was only one of the many houses where the boys slept together in Mwanalilenji. There were also several *kuka,* girls' dormitories, where Apasani's sisters and their agemates retired every evening. Both boys and girls left their *gowero* or *kuka* only when they got married.

"Chosadziwa," Apasani said as they entered the *gowero,* "you sleep next to me on this mat. The slave can sleep over there." He pointed to a corner in the gloom. The only light was from the fire one of the boys had lit earlier. Apasani sat on a tree-stump by the fireside. Some of the other boys did the same. Others sat on their mats. Again, Chosadziwa was the centre of attraction.

"Don't they tell stories before going to sleep in Maitsalani?" invited Apasani.

"They do." Chosadziwa took the cue. "But first, the riddles."

"Of course."

"Ndugi." Chosadziwa was enjoying himself. "Riddle! Riddle!"

"Jize," chorused the rest. "Let it come! Let it come!"

Dzunzo leaned against the wall in his corner. He had always enjoyed the riddling and storytelling sessions with his Maitsalani cousins. He discovered that everyone grew up with more or less the same riddles and stories, until someone learned a new one from elsewhere. Chosadziwa's repertoire had attracted the Maitsalani boys' admiration, since he had brought an entirely new set of riddles and stories not only from his own village but also from the hunters. The most difficult ones to crack were the travellers' riddles.

"When I went visiting, I was greeted from afar."

"A *mwiyo* bird."

"No."

"A *mwichire* bird."

"No."

"You have failed," Chosadziwa said triumphantly. Dzunzo knew the answer, of course, but could not say a word. "What are you going to give me for the answer?"

"Father's chickens."

"That's not enough."

"His rice fields."

"That's not enough."

"Cousin, you haven't seen his fields yet."

41

"All right," Chosadziwa relented. "I'll be satisfied with that wealth. The answer is 'dogs'. It's still my turn to throw another riddle. Riddle! Riddle!"

"Let it come!"

"I went visiting. They spread a mat for me, but the first to sit on it were kids. What is it?"

"Water!"

"Your shadow!"

They went through the same ritual of symbolic transfer of wealth to Chosadziwa.

"I'm going to inherit the whole village," Chosadziwa crowed. "Mwanalilenji will be mine! The answer is 'flies'."

"A story! Now stories!" chorused some of the boys, having exhausted themselves.

"You start."

"No, the strangers start."

"No," Chosadziwa protested. "Let's hear one from the owners of the village first."

"All right," Apasani volunteered.

He told the "Chifane-fane" ("Identical Twins") story. There was a couple. The husband had a twin who lived in a distant land. The twin had heard that his brother was now married, so he came to meet his sister-in-law. The husband warned his wife that they were identical twins, and everyone, including her, would mistake one for the other. The wife claimed that after living with him for so long, she, of all people, could not mistake him for another person. One day, while the husband was away, the twin arrived. The wife thought he was her husband. The twin tried to correct her, but she insisted that he was her husband, pretending to be the twin. She prepared a hot bath for him, then the evening meal, all the while asking her husband to drop the pretence. The twin meanwhile kept to his story. When bedtime came, she was surprised he refused to share the same space with her. The real husband found them arguing about fulfilling conjugal duties.

"The wife was stupid," Chosadziwa commented at the end. "How could she be so easily duped?"

"It's your turn now," Apasani said as he finished.

"Since you're telling stories about pretending," Chosadziwa started, "I'll tell you one from the mountains. Once upon a time ..."

"We're together."

"... the hyena fell in love."

"We're together." Giggling.

"Seriously," Chosadziwa interposed, "this hideous hyena, on one of his travels, came upon a beautiful woman by a river like Mzimundilinde."

"We're together."

"He said to himself, 'What shall I do? One does not negotiate one's own marriage. The relatives will say, "Don't you have a *nkhoswe* to come and speak for you?" Now who shall I ask to be the go-between? I can't ask my fellow hyenas. They're as ugly as me.' You see, the hyena had just followed her discreetly from the river to find out which village she came from and which house she lived in."

"We're together."

"After he had found out these facts, he started looking around for a go-between. Kalulu the Hare found him in this state.

"You look so miserable,' Kalulu asked the hyena, 'what are you thinking about?' You know Kalulu and Fisi are sometimes enemies, sometimes friends. This time they were not quarrelling. In fact, they hadn't met for some time."

"We're together."

"Ah, Kalulu, my friend,' Fisi said, 'the very person I'm looking for!'

"Me? Why?' asked Kalulu.

"I need your help.'

"You know me, Fisi.' Kalulu sat down next to him. 'You can trust me. What is it?'

"In Takoma Village,' Fisi confided, 'there's a woman by the name of Chiphetsa. I'm in love with her. Pm dying to marry her.'

"So, what's stopping you?'

"I need a *nkhoswe*.'

"You want me to be your *nkhoswe* ?'

"'Please, if you can.'

"Of course I can. You know my sweet tongue. Even if she didn't love you, I could convince her to agree to marry you. Have you talked to her?'

No.'

"What about her people?'

"You know our customs. I can't negotiate on my own behalf.'

"You mean she's never seen you? And her people don't know

you?'

"Not yet.'

"That's no problem. I'll go on your behalf. I'd do anything for a friend, especially one who's in love.'

"Thank you, my friend.'

"Kalulu went to Takoma, to Chiphetsa's house, as directed. But do you know what?"

"No! Tell us!"

"'He, too, fell in love with Chiphetsa!"

"No! So what happened?"

"He went to Chiphetsa and declared his love."

"Directly?"

44

"Of course. You're allowed to do that."

"Then what'?"

"Chiphetsa told him to come the following day so she could introduce him to her people. Kalulu agreed, and told her, 'Tomorrow you'll see me again, but not on foot. I'll be riding my horse.'

"Oh, so you've got a horse?'

"Yes! I'm rich!'

"Now, we come to the interesting part." Chosadziwa interrupted himself. "Kalulu went back to the hyena.

"How did it go, my friend?'

"Fine. No problem. Chiphetsa has agreed.'

"You talked to her?'

"Of course I did. I had to get her consent before proceeding. How could I just go ahead with *unkhoswe* without it?'

"You're right. And she agreed?'

"She agreed. Man, she's dying to see you. She can't wait to get married. She says tomorrow we must go together to meet her uncles, aunts, and all that.'

"I know. I can't wait, either. The girl is just too beautiful to leave single. Aren't there any men in Takoma? Don't they see her?'

"I wondered the same when I set eyes on her.'

"Let's start getting ready for our visit.'

"The two of them discussed how they would proceed."

"We're together."

"The following day, they put on their best clothes."

"We're together."

"They walked and walked. They crossed the river, but when they neared the village, Kalulu fell sick."

45

"No!"

"He did — terribly sick! 'I can't go on,' he said.

"But you must!' Fisi insisted.

"I feel faint.' Kalulu nearly collapsed.

"Fisi was frantic. 'We're nearly there, just four hundred yards.'

"I can't manage unless you carry me.'

"We've got to see this through together. You're the only one who can help me. Come, get on my back. I hope you can at least talk.'

"Once I get there, I can speak on your behalf.'

"Kalulu got onto Fisi's back. They entered the village like that, with Kalulu straddling Fisi's back and holding onto his shoulders."

"We're together."

"Chiphetsa and her relatives were waiting for them on the *khonde.* As they neared the house, Kalulu took a rope from his pocket and put it across Fisi's mouth, like a halter."

"Look!' Kalulu shouted to the people. 'My horse!'

"Fisi realised too late that he had been tricked. He sprang up on his hind legs to run away. Kalulu jumped off just in time. He joined the group on the *khonde* and waited to be introduced to his future in-laws "

"The trickster!" chortled some of the younger boys.

"I haven't heard that one before!" Apasani chimed in. "The elders say it's the stranger who has a sharp razor!"

"In this case, a sharp tongue," pointed out one of the cousins.

"How true!" thought Dzunzo grudgingly. He had heard the story from the same tongue before. He wanted to add, "The greatest trickster is the storyteller himself. He's the one who changed the roles in the real story," but what came out was merely grunts and groans. The group just looked at him, amused, whether by the story they had just heard or his condition he could not tell.

46

An owl hooted on the roof of the *gowero.*

"That's ominous." Apasani looked round the group. He pushed some wood into the middle of the fire. Sparks flew.

"Something's going to happen tomorrow." Chosadziwa's face gleamed in the dying light.

"I wonder what."

"Not a death, I hope."

"Don't be so gloomy. We haven't heard of any illnesses."

"Then someone is going to fall sick."

"Maybe the slave." Chosadziwa chuckled, looking in Dzunzo's direction. "He looks sick enough."

"Yes," Apasani agreed. "He must be homesick!"

Everyone laughed looking at Dzunzo's wretched form. "Ph— Th— Ng."

"Yes, he's agreeing. He's homesick." This brought more bursts of laughter.

"Aah," Apasani cocked his head to one side. "At least that's not as ominous."

The boys all listened with him. In the distance, the nightjar sang of the night, *"Let the moon shine so we can eat tadpoles."*

"On that note," Apasani signalled to the rest, "let's go to sleep."

The boys went to their mats. Apasani pulled the last log off the fire, so it would not light up again. Dzunzo was still leaning against the wall in the corner, but everyone ignored him. In any case, they could no longer see him. It seemed he was the only one left awake to listen to the owl's *"Who? Who?"* and the nightjar's *"Let the moon shine so we can eat tadpoles."*

47

Chapter Six

The Bird Boy's Song

Four doors away from the boys' *gowelo,* Mlauzi and Nalichowa went over the day's events. Guilt lay heavily on them, more especially on Mlauzi, Naliyela's brother, than Nalichowa, who was only a sister-in-law. All the same, she too felt strongly about Naliyela.

"We should ... I should have gone to Maitsalani after the *chitengwa,*" Mlauzi mused in bed. "Even if we had more or less sold Naliyela to Ndasauka, it did not mean we had to sever all contact with her and her adopted people."

"Maitsalani is too far away for casual visits."

"At least for the outdooring ceremony or even the naming. These are not casual events. The naming was our right. I wonder who named the boy Chosadziwa."

"It's a strange name: he who does not know, the ignorant one."

"Why would anyone give him that name? He looks quite intelligent. Look how he found his way here. And with an epileptic slave."

"How did they cross the flooded Mzimundilinde?"

"Exactly. A fool and one who doesn't know the crossing could not have done it. And he's just a boy, really."

"We missed the outdooring ceremony, the naming ceremony, but the most serious is the funeral ceremony. They should have sent us word of Naliyela's death."

"Yet they didn't."

"Doesn't that strike you as strange?"

"Maybe the Maitsalani people take *chitengwa* literally. After the exchange of goods and person they sever all ties. We made it worse by not following it up with visits just to keep up relationships between the two villages."

48

"I don't mind their keeping Ndasauka's death a secret but my sister ... not to mourn her."

"We should have a *sadaka* then."

"Yes, after the joy of recovering our little nephew."

"We should get more details of her death. We were so overjoyed at Chosadziwa's coming we did not enquire more into the deaths of his parents."

"Chosadziwa is the messenger of the two deaths."

"He is more than that."

"What do you mean?"

"It means we can't go to Maitsalani now to claim any of Naliyela's property in spite of the *chitengwa*. It means anything that Chosadziwa inherited from his father is also forfeited."

"Surely not his rightful inheritance. He is entitled to a share of his father's wealth. You can at least chase the Maitsalani people up on that".

"Any other people, yes, we could have negotiated with, but not the Maitsalani people."

"What do you mean?"

"Look," Mlauzi sat up in his bed. "What kind of people would chase their nephew, yes, their own son, away from the village soon after his parents' death? You see the kind of people we're dealing with?"

Mlauzi thought back to the *chitengwa* ceremony. Of course, the *ankhoswe* from Maitsalani had come. They had stayed for a week on Mwanalilenji's hospitality. Not that it was strained: Mwanalilenji was well-named: there had been a week of feasting, eating and drinking. Several relationships had been established. He remembered some of the names: Madala and Mdoda. Was it Mdoda who almost turned the *chitengwa* into a double wedding? But after striking up a relationship with Mlauzi's other sister, he had not followed it up. Perhaps the whole ceremony had been hollow. Perhaps the lack of follow-up could be blamed on both parties. But to banish the boy was really the ultimate sign of shallow relationships. Was

49

chitengwa a realistic custom? Did Ndasauka really love Naliyela? What had their married life been like after the couple had been given a rousing send off from Mwanalilenji? There were a lot of things he wanted to know about his sister, about his brother-in-law, about Maitsalani.

"I see how difficult it is now," Nalichowa echoed Mlauzi's thoughts, "to resume any relationship with our in-laws."

"Where would we start? Whose court would settle a dispute of this kind? Ours or theirs?"

"We can't go to theirs, and I'm sure they won't come to ours, either."

"We must probe our nephew more deeply. We need to know more about Maitsalani."

The couple slept on that.

They woke up early the next day to the persistent call of the tailor bird: *"Grab your hoe! Get to work!"* The bird was wrong. It was not time for hoeing but for harvesting Mlauzi and Nalichowa ate their morning meal, *kadzutsa,* and got ready for cutting down the rice in the fields.

Apasani, Lekadala and the other sons found their parents with their *namagwape* sickles. Chosadziwa was with them. Dzunzo was in tow. He did not know what to do now, especially with his speech impediment.

"How did you sleep, my nephew?" Mlauzi greeted Chosadziwa affably.

"It's great to be with my cousins."

"He's a great storyteller," Bengo said eagerly.

"And a great tiddler!" Limbani joined in.

"So you had a session." Mlauzi laughed. "Well, no storytelling during the day. Too much work to do. After you've eaten, you boys go to the platform by the graveyard. The *mpheta* roost in those graveyard trees. We'll be harvesting on the other side of the garden."

After their *kadzutsa,* Apasani and Lekadala, the older boys, led the rest to their appointed posts in the rice fields. Chosadziwa and Dzunzo retraced the path they had taken the previous day, skirting the graveyard and reaching the first field. The *mpheta* birds were already there, swarming around. Chosadziwa recognised most of the different birds: weavers, waxbills, sparrows, warblers, widow birds, and more tailor birds. He knew there would be other ground birds in the fields and the forest: francolins and guinea fowl. The *machete* birds wove their nests around *nsangu* tree branches.

"I've never seen so many birds in one spot anywhere else," commented Chosadziwa.

"We kill them by the hundreds, too," Apasani said. "We sometimes come out at night with *ukonde* nets and just wrap them up."

"I'm used to *ulimbo, khwekwe* and *diwa* traps," Chosadziwa announced.

"We use them too, but only for the big ground birds. With *khwekwe* or *diwa* you can only catch one bird at a time."

Dzunzo remembered Chosadziwa teaching him to set a *khwekwe* for guinea fowl, or tap *nkhadzi* trees like the ones around Mwanalilenji graveyard for bird lime. You could catch three or four birds at a time with bird lime, before the rest of the swarm got wise.

"Chosadziwa and your slave," Apasani instructed the strangers, "you stay on this platform. I'll be on the next. Lekadala will be at the corner, and so on."

The platforms rested on rolled tree stumps. The floor was made of bamboo poles tied closely together. There was a grass roof on top to keep out the rain. Chosadziwa and Dzunzo climbed to their platform. They could see rice fields spread out in front of them right up to the trees of Mzimundilinde. Interspersed at short intervals were scarecrows that fluttered in the breeze. Only a few birds were fooled by their fluttering. They came back again and again to settle on the rice stalks, after fleeing a few feet away.

"Now, slave!" Chosadziwa taunted Dzunzo, "do your work!"

Before Dzunzo could respond, a bird sang from the *thundu* tree in the graveyard:

Guku, you have rejected your own child!

51

You have rejected your own child, guku!

Then Dzunzo's throat relaxed. Out came a song he had never sung before:

Psya! Birds!
Mother used to tell me
When I die
Go to my relatives
Kadimba and his wife Luli
Psya! Birds!

Immediately all the birds fled from Mlauzi's field below them. Chosadziwa gasped and shuddered violently. The spell had been broken, so soon! He went weak at the knees. He felt nerveless. He leaned on the nearest pole for support, but slipped and fell. He rolled on the floor, groaning as if in great pain. His face went into a spasm. He saw the results of his deception looming.

*   *   *   *   *   *   *

Mlauzi and Nalichowa were at the bottom of the field, cutting the rice stalks, tying them up in bundles, and stacking them at a distance, ready for carrying home. Rice-growing was taxing. Farmers had to tend the rice from planting to eating. Mlauzi and Nalichowa had transplanted the sprouted seeds in the water-logged fields in the rainy season. Then they had weeded regularly until the harvest, when nadanga weeds, which closely resembled rice, competed with the genuine crop. Between planting and harvesting, they had to keep beetles, grasshoppers, crickets, moths and their maggots and caterpillars away from the stalks, in addition to watching out for blight and brown spot. The rodents started coming early on, the swimmers among them coming with the first rains, the *kapuku*, *mfuko* and others coming towards harvest time. These ate roots, stalks and grain. Harvest time brought *machete*, *mpheta*, *phingo* birds, which needed to be chased away by teams of children and their parents. After harvesting they had to keep the weevils and rats out of the *nkhokwe*. As the elders said, the only rice they could be assured of was what they were chewing. The rest was at the mercy of other forces they had to battle against throughout the year.

Apart from all these pests, rice-growers had to keep a constant check on the weather. Water they certainly needed in abundance. This they got from Mzimundilinde, which never dried up, and from the rains. In the rainy season, the problem was how to control it. There were times when *Napolo,* the harbinger of floods, had descended from Mtalika mountains and washed away everything in his path: rice, sorghum, trees, houses, animals and humans. However, over time, the people built great bunds to control the fury of the underground serpent. They directed the water into channels leading deeper and deeper into the gardens, thus dissipating much of the force of the floods. Now, in times when *Napolo* was particularly fierce, only the fields nearest the river would suffer, but the owners had other plots on the plains.

These thoughts had all been passing through Mlauzi's mind when he caught the bird song from the graveyard. Husband and wife paused in their work.

"What kind of bird is that?"

"When it says *'guku* it sounds like a pigeon."

"It can't be *njiwa !"*

"Listen!"

Up in the *thundu* tree, the bird started again:

> Guku, *you've rejected your own child!*
> *You've rejected your own child, guku!*

"What is it saying?"

"You've rejected your own child!"

"What does it mean?"

"Listen to the boy singing now."

From the platform, the boy sang again:

> *Psya! Birds!*
> *Mother used to tell me*
> *When I die*

Go to my relatives
Kadimba and his wife Luli
Psya! Birds!

"That's not Chosadziwa. It's not his voice."

"It must be the slave boy."

"It can't be. He's mute."

"But he's only singing when the bird leads him."

The song floated hauntingly across the rice paddies. The birds all fled into the trees.

"But he's singing about us."

"How did he know our real names?"

"Chosadziwa only called us by our clan names. This boy is calling us by our navel names."

"Let's go and find out."

They came upon Dzunzo on the platform. He was singing sorrowfully to the birds, tears streaming down his cheeks. The other boys had also left their platforms to listen to him.

"Stop!" Mlauzi shouted at him. "Who are you?"

"I'm Dzunzo," Dzunzo surprised himself. He could speak again at last!

"What happened to you?"

"Chosadziwa cast a spell on me. He deceived you. Oh, how he duped you!"

"You're confusing us."

"Chosadziwa is the slave. I'm your true nephew, Naliyela's son, from Maitsalani. Mother told me your real names, Kadimba and Luli. Chosadziwa only knew the clan names. I had told him them!"

"This is incredible!" Mlauzi looked closely at Dzunzo. "Where is Chosadziwa?"

"Hiding under the platform!"

"Get out from there, you wretch!" Mlauzi stomped on the wooden platform. Apasani and Lekadala jumped down, squatted and peered underneath.

"You heard my father," Apasani shouted at a form in the shadows. "If you don't come out we'll get you ourselves and you'll regret it."

"I already regret what I've done." Chosadziwa crawled into the open on his stomach.

"Already regret? Did you hear this boy say regret? You don't know what great wrong you have done me, Dzunzo and the whole village. You say you regret ...?"

"Forgive me!" Chosadziwa squatted on his haunches like a frog but did not stand up. "I know it is a great crime."

"How could you plot to kill my nephew like this?" Mlauzi descended upon the boy. The boy shrank back, clasping his hands before his eyes. Apasani and Lekadala stood over him, one on each side, incredulity and disgust written on their faces.

"Leave him to us!" Apasani glowered at Chosadziwa.

"We'll deal with him" Lekadala prowled round the slave.

"He's a wizard" Nalichowa said at last. "Only a sorcerer could have such a hardened spleen to commit such a crime to his fellow human being."

"Tie him up," Mlauzi ordered.

Apasani and Lekadala did as their father instructed. Bengo and Dumbo giggled.

"Now you know what it is like to be tied up." Lekadala pushed Chosadziwa, who rolled on the ground.

"What are you going to do with him?" Dzunzo asked.

"He can't live with us anymore," Apasani said.

"He'll kill us all with his magic," Lekadala concluded.

The bird crooned from the graveyard:

Guku, *you have rejected your own child!*
You have rejected your own child, guku!

"What's this bird that's singing?"

"It's up there in the *thundu* tree," Dzunzo volunteered. "That's where Chosadziwa cast the spell on me."

"Let's get there quickly."

Mlauzi and Nalichowa led the way. Dzunzo was between them. Apasani pulled Chosadziwa to his feet. Between him and Lekadala, they pushed Chosadziwa along. The rest followed, through the other rice fields, shrubs and grasses.

They crowded under the *thundu* tree. Something fluttered high up in the branches.

Guku, *you have rejected your own child!*
You have rejected your own child, guku!

"I can't see it," Nalichowa said.

"It sounds like a *namalinda* or a *narnada,*" Mlauzi hazarded.

"That can't be a parrot," Nalichowa objected. "It sounds like a human being. It's ghostly." Her voice had become subdued.

"What did Chosadziwa do to you?" Mlauzi turned to Dzunzo.

"He took earth from this mound and sprinkled it on my head and mouth, and suddenly I was struck dumb."

"You mean you could talk before this?"

"I was normal till we reached this point. That boy is a magician."

"If you're our true son," Mlauzi declared solemnly, "then you're standing on your village founder's mound."

"That's what Chosadziwa said."

"Then your ancestor has saved you."

56

"That must be his spirit up there," Mlauzi pointed. "Come, let's get away from here. We've disturbed the ancestors enough."

"I told you," Nalichowa started wailing again. "The people from the grave do come back. They came back to tell us the truth about our son here."

"Chosadziwa, you will be punished for this." Mlauzi led the way out of the graveyard.

Chapter Seven

Child of the Wild

Evening came, and it was Dzunzo's turn to be feasted, this time on goat meat and rice. Mlauzi and Nalichowa excelled themselves as if to make amends all in one night. Now it was Dzunzo's turn to recount his adventures and life in Maitsalani. Uncle and aunt probed, dissected and put together all the pieces of information Dzunzo gave them. Chosadziwa was thrown into an empty rice granary still tied up, so he couldn't escape. They released Dzunzo to sleep with his cousins at the *gowelo* and retired for the night. In bed Mlauzi and Nalichowa reviewed the day's events.

"I don't know what Dzunzo feels about us," Mlauzi lamented aloud. "He came here looking for his relatives. He expected his uncle and aunt to receive him well, comfort him on his banishment and bereavement. He came to us as his second parents and what did we do to him? We turned him into something worse than an orphan: he was a slave in his own home!"

"It wasn't entirely our fault," Nalichowa corrected her husband. "Chosadziwa had already turned him into a slave before we set eyes on him."

"I'm the father of four sons and three daughters. I've seen all seven of them grow up under my close supervision. I know when they're lying and when they're telling the truth. How could I have believed Chosadziwa's story just like that?"

"But how could you not have believed him? You had no evidence to the contrary. Dzunzo was mute, tied up and presumed epileptic. Who could have told us the truth?"

"But even Apasani or Lekadala would not have believed Chosadziwa if I had not already accepted the slave's story. Without my gullibility, they could have punched holes in his story, and even his behaviour."

"What do you mean?"

"Granted that Dzunzo was mute. He himself admitted that the impediment was there. But epilepsy is another thing. At my age I should know how an epileptic behaves. Look at the way Chosadziwa held Dzunzo down yesterday on the *khonde*. Is that the way epileptics behave? Even if Dzunzo was afflicted, how could Chosadziwa have travelled with an epileptic all this distance from Maitsalani to Mwanalilenji, and Mzimundilinde in flood too?"

"Stop blaming yourself. I'm to blame, as well. I, too, was taken in by the story. I didn't even think to enquire too closely into the epilepsy story. In fact we ignored Dzunzo as soon as we were told he was a slave. We focused on Chosadziwa, whom we took to be our nephew. We enjoyed his company as much as he enjoyed ours. Yes, let's admit it. He was literally enjoying us too, in his duplicity."

"Maybe we're getting too old. We were too trusting. Look at the matter of names. Anyone, even a child, knows us by our clan names, Mlauzi and Nalichowa. It's the custom for addressing elders. I ... we ... should have probed the wretch and asked him to give us our proper names."

"But there was no reason to distrust him. We had never seen our nephew before. He came out of the wilds to introduce himself as our nephew. What else could we say or do but believe him?"

"After being cut off from my sister for so long, why should I accept the first impostor that shows his face here?"

"Look, things are all right now. Your true nephew has been recognised. The murderer, yes, he's a murderer, has been caught. He's going to die for his sins."

"Yes, death is the only punishment appropriate for his sins. Let's sleep on it."

*   *   *   *   *   *   *

Four houses away Dzunzo was also going through agonies over the day's events. There were several memorable incidents, the greatest being the release of his vocal chords to be able to speak and sing again. This was followed by the triumphal procession back into the village as the genuine nephew. The feast of goat meat and rice was the culminating point of the happy turn of events. Yet something kept gnawing at him: the fate of Chosadziwa. This morning's interrogation scene leapt wildly into his mind. There was Mlauzi looking terrible. And there was Chosadziwa cringing before the old man.

"As Maitsalani people banished you and my nephew from their village, I can't have you here. This is the least punishment I can devise for you after what you have done to Dzunzo, me, and my people."

"If you banish me from here, where will I go? I longed to have a home, I pined for a mother and someone to call father but they were denied me from an early age."

"From what I hear, my sister and brother-in-law gave you a home in Maitsalani. They gave you the love of a mother and father but you chose to abuse it."

"All these were foster this or foster that: foster mother, foster father, foster home. I have nothing that is mine by birth."

"The child," Nalichowa came in, "speaks the wisdom of an adult. These are the words of one who has lived through deep pain and thought about it for long."

"He is the stuff witches are made of," Mlauzi argued. "At his age he couldn't have planned to usurp his master's place the way he did, coming to Mwanalilenji. He shouldn't be banished — he should be killed."

The adults had left it at that. During the festivities that followed, Chosadziwa was not mentioned, Dzunzo wondered if he had even been given a meal.

As he had done on the road to Mwanalilenji, Dzunzo considered again the good and bad points of his "blood brother". Dzunzo knew that Chosadziwa indeed had a cruel streak in him. Some of the things he did seemed senseless. Take the *ehelule* incident for example. Chosadziwa had lured the harmless little bird to sleep with his chant:

Chelule, *go to sleep!* Chelule, *go to sleep!*

The foolish bird had dozed on its branch and fallen asleep. All Chosadziwa had done was to pick it up. He had wanted to pluck it and eat it, but Dzunzo had protested. The thing was so tiny it couldn't satisfy anyone, so why kill it? Chosadziwa had reluctantly freed the bird.

Some of Chosadziwa's acts were double-edged: both destructive and creative. Take the case of the *nkhumbu.* Again Chosadziwa had brought it down with a chant:

Nkhumbu, *alight here!*
At your home there's no tree!
Nkhumbu, *alight here!*

The insect had fluttered, its hard outer wings crackling, and it had finally landed. Chosadziwa had killed and roasted it. He had plucked off the wings, making it obvious that he had done the same thing to dozens of others of these tiny insects. He had produced over a dozen of the wings. He had pierced a hole in the top of each wing, pulled a string through them and created a musical instrument. He had tied the ends of the string to each of his toes and stretched his feet apart. He had plucked the taut string with his fingers and the wings had produced a high or low-pitched sound according to their size. He had sung an attractive fast-paced accompaniment:

Macherechete, *escort me outside!*
I want to relieve myself!
What about the pitch darkness?
I will kick it away.

Dzunzo had been fascinated by the words of the song, especially the idea of the feet kicking away the dark.

Dzunzo was reminded of the pitch darkness that must have enveloped Chosadziwa even during the day when he was shut in the rice granary. He looked up from his mat. In the gloom he could make out the sleeping forms of his cousins. After the day's events and the festivities they had passed out. They had not even had the energy to have a story-telling session.

Dzunzo got up, stealthily picking up his clothes on the way. He picked his way carefully between the other mats. He reached the door without stepping on anyone. The grass door made only the faintest whisper as he pulled it aside. He shut it again behind him. He put on his clothes and stepped out in the direction of his uncle's compound. The moon was up and he could make out the shapes of the main house, kitchen and bath shacks. The granaries were like miniature huts, yet big enough for several human beings to be kept inside.

No, Dzunzo thought as he paused in his walk, Chosadziwa was not entirely evil. Dzunzo owed him everything he knew about bird, insect and animal lore; he had learned the uses of common trees and shrubs from him; Chosadziwa had told him everything the Maitsalani children and adults could not. He had been a good companion until they had reached Mzimundilinde.

Dzunzo made out the empty granary in the dark. It was the second of the four that stood in a row behind Mlauzi's compound. Like all granaries, it had a platform one stood on to pour in the rice without having to get inside once the roof was raised. Dzunzo raised the roof with a pole he found nearby.

"Who is it?" came a tired, frightened voice.

"It's me. Keep quiet!"

Dzunzo climbed the wooden ladder leaning against the granary. At the top, he put one leg over, then the other. He had to cling to the top of the granary to lower himself inside.

"Where are you?"

"Here!"

Dzunzo felt his way with his hands to the prostrate form. He felt all over him for the ropes.

"What are you doing?"

"Freeing you, stupid!" He found a knot and unravelled it.

"Why?"

"You've got to get out of this place." Another knot.

"I told you I haven't got anywhere to go."

"Do you want to die?"

"I don't think your uncle would go to the extent of killing me." He was now sitting upright and helped to undo the rest of the knots he only could feel in the dark.

"After what you did to him? To me? To us? Don't fool yourself. If he doesn't kill you, it will be something equally painful. You know how children are disposed of in ritual places?"

"What am I going to do?" They were now standing side by side.

"Go back to Maitsalani."

"I can't! You know that." He stepped away from Dzunzo.

"It's the only safe place. They might have banished me because of my parents. They can't banish you because you were never one of us. The least they can do is to take you back as a slave."

"Never! No one will make me a slave again! I was only your father's slave because he rescued me from those elephant hunters. I was your slave because I grew to love you, too. You are the only companion I ever knew. I am not going back to servitude."

"So what are you going to do?"

"I'm a creature of the wild. That's where I learned to live and survive on nature. I lived for years with the hunters learning the secrets of mountains, forests and rivers."

Chosadziwa had demonstrated his knowledge of the wilds in many ways to Dzunzo. He had played hide-and-seek with him. Chosadziwa could never be caught. He could make himself look like a boulder or a tree-stump, if he wished.

"I'm giving you the opportunity to go back to the mountains, forests, and rivers. That's where you really belong."

"That's home to me. What's going to happen to you?"

"This is where I belong. I'll become a boy of the rice and sorghum fields."

"They will know you cut me loose."

"Let's not waste time. You must put a great distance between you and them before dawn, just in case they chase after you."

"They wanted to banish me in the first place"

"I know. I'll explain to them why I freed you."

"Thanks for everything." Chosadziwa hugged Dzunzo. Dzunzo responded. Chosadziwa freed himself. Dzunzo heard him heave himself up, slither over the top and pad down the rungs outside. Then silence.

Slowly Dzunzo followed Chosadziwa's example. Outside he paused to replace the roof on the granary. He stepped back down on the ground. As he retraced his steps to the boys' *gowe to* , Dzunzo knew even if his uncle sent anyone, the people of the rice fields could not capture Chosadziwa.

"I'm not going back into slavery," Chosadziwa had said. "I'm a creature of the wild."

- The End -

Glossary

Most vernacular words are translated within the text immediately after they occur. However, for the benefit of those who would like to have translations at a glance, they also appear below:

Aah! Mbalame!	literally, "Ah! Birds!" — a bird-scarer's shout.
adzukulu	group of people, not related to the bereaved family, who prepare the corpse for burial (not to be confused with *adzukulu* — nephews or nieces — (sg. mdzukulu).
alendo	visitors (sg. *mlendo*).
Alendo siyawo	literally "Visitors — there they are!" — a bird; also its song.
chelule	type of bird.
chifane-fane	that which is identical. In this story, the title of the folktale about identical twins.
chikande	ground or mashed root from a plant used as relish.
chisoso	type of wild vegetable.
chitengwa	in a patrilineal society, the custom allowing a woman to leave her home to live in her husband's village. (See also *mtengwa*.)
chitimbe	type of tree.
chiwamba	roasted meat stored for future consumption at home or on a journey.
diwa	trap which releases a rock to crush the animal or bird when the bait is taken.
dimba	garden near a river or on marshland, usually for growing vegetables.
faya	type of cultivated rice.
gowero	boys' sleeping place or dormitory.
gugu	type of wild grass which resembles rice.
guku	chirp of the pigeon.

Jize!	literally "Let it come!" — the response to "*Ndagi!*" (riddle), per-mitting the riddler to proceed.
kachere	type of tree.
kadzutsa	the morning meal.
kamba	food taken to eat on a long journey (not to be confused with *kamba* — tortoise).
kamphe	type of grass.
kapuku	fieldmouse.
khonde	verandah or raised platform around house or granary.
khwekwe	ground trap which uses string loop to capture the victim.
kuka	girls' sleeping place or dormitory.
macherechete	(plural) the hard wings of the *nkhumbu* insect, when strung together to make a musical instrument
machete	type of bird.
masau	type of wild fruit
masuku	type of wild fruit.
mateme	type of wild fruit.
mfuko	mole.
mgodo	uncooked rice mash.
mkate	traditional African bread.
mlombwa	mahogany tree.
mpheta	type of bird.
mpinjipinji	type of tree.
mpoza	wild custard apple.
mtengwa	in a patrilineal society, the woman who leaves her home to live in her husband's village, according to the custom of *chitengwa*.
mvunguti	sausage tree.
mwichire	type of bird. "*Mwichire kamba*" — its song: literally "Leave out food for the visitors".

mwiyo	type of bird.
nadanga	weeds which closely resemble rice.
namada	talking bird, like a parrot.
natnalinda	talking bird, like a parrot.
namgwape	type of sickle.
Napolo	mythical underground serpent associated with floods, earthquakes, storms, etc.
ndagi	riddle. Also the opening formula for a riddle session.
ndiwo	relish.
njenjereretu	choral response to bird-scarer's song in the story.
njiwa	pigeon.
nkhadzi	type of tree.
nkhoswe	go-between for a marriage or a married couple; counsellor — from either side of the family. *Unkhoswe* — actual negotiation involving *ankhoswe* (plural).
nkhumbu	type of flying insect.
nsangu	type of tree.
nsenjere	type of river grass.
nsima	hard porridge made from grain.
nthudza	type of wild fruit.
phingo	type of bird.
phwiti	type of bird.
Psya!	like "*Aah!*" — bird-scarer's shout.
sadaka	ritual meal commemorating the dead.
sichilile	type of wild grass which resembles rice.
therere	wild leaves used as relish, also okra.
thobwa	non-alcoholic drink made from grain.
thundu	type of tree.
ukonde	net used to catch birds or fish.
ulimbo	bird lime.

Appendix I

The Orphan and the Slave

as told to the author by **Akubwalula**

There was a certain man and his wife who had an only son. The parents advised him that when they died he should go back to their original village beyond the lake. He should go and live with the parents' relatives: Kadimba and his wife Luli.

After a time, the parents died. They left only a slave as a companion to their son. The two boys decided to follow the parents' advice and go to live with Kadimba and Luli. They packed all their belongings and started on their journey. On the way, they found that the river they had to cross was flooded.

"Give me your clothes," the slave said, "and I will ferry them over to the other side. You can take the luggage."

The boy agreed. The slave took the boy's clothes and put them on, leaving the freeborn with the rags and the luggage. They both crossed safely to the other side of the river.

"Now that we have crossed the river," the boy said, "there is the luggage for you to carry. Give me back my clothes."

The slave told him that he would do that by and by. They went on. Every so often the boy reminded the slave to return the clothes and carry the luggage. The slave kept answering that he would do so eventually. This went on until the two travellers reached their destination.

The people received them happily. They spread a mat for the slave to sit on, while the freeborn, who was still in rags, was ordered to sit in the bush. The villagers slaughtered a cow for the slave and gave him choice pieces, while the freeborn was given the leftovers to eat with *nsima* made from maize husk flour.

These people grew rice, and when the grain ripened, the fields were ravaged by birds. They gave the freeborn the work of scaring the birds away, while the slave was feasted and given an honoured place in the village.

When birds came to the field the boy watched over, he used to sing the following song:

> *Aah! Aah! Birds, njenjereretu*
> *Mother used to tell me, njenjereretu*
> *When I die, njenjereretu*
> *Go to my relatives, njenjereretu*
> *Kadimba and his wife Lull, njenjereretu*
> *Aah! Aah! Birds, njenjereretu*

When the birds heard the song, they used to leave his field alone and attack the others.

There was a graveyard nearby, and when the boy finished his song, a bird responded from there:

> *Guku, you have rejected your own child!*
> *You have rejected your own child, guku!*

The other bird-scarers, who had their shacks near the boy, noted and wondered at all this. They went home. And when the birds came, he sang the same song again:

> *Ault! Ault! Birds, njenjereretu*
> *Mother used to tell me, njenjereretu*
> *When I die, njenjereretu*
> *Go to my relatives, njenjereretu*
> *Kadimba and his wife Lull, njenjereretu*
> *Aah! Aah! Birds, njenjereretu*

Immediately he finished his song, the same response came from the graveyard:

> *Guku, you have rejected your own child!*
> *You have rejected your own child, guku!*

The other bird-scarers were mystified, and went to tell Kadimba and Luli what they had seen and heard.

"What our friend sings at the fields," they said, "is very strange. He sings a song and no bird comes to his field. The song talks about how when his mother died he was told to go to Kadimba and Luli. As soon as he finishes singing his song, a bird replies from the graveyard with another song about a child that has been rejected."

Kadimba and his wife were amazed. "He actually mentions our names in the song?" they asked.

"Yes," was the answer.

"Well then," Kadimba announced, "tomorrow we will go together to the fields to see for ourselves."

Next morning, Kadimba and Luli followed at a safe distance, so that the boy would not know. They reached the fields and the birds came again. The boy sang his song again:

> *Aah! Aah! Birds, njenjereretu*
> *Mother used to tell me, njenjereretu*
> *When I die, njenjereretu*
> *Go to my relatives, njenjereretu*
> *Kadimba and his wife Luli, njenjereretu*
> *Aah! Aah! Birds, njenjereretu*

Immediately after the song, a bird answered from the graveyard:

> *Guku, you have rejected your own child!*
> *You have rejected your own child, guku!*

The boy's relatives were chilled through and through. Kadimba and his wife rushed on to the platform the boy was watching from. They wept over him, with Luli rolling on the ground in great grief. They realised that they had ill-treated their own child and honoured a worthless slave.

Kadimba carried the boy home on his back. They took hold of the slave and tore him to pieces for deceiving them. They took the pieces and threw them into the river. This is where the story ended.

Printed in the United States
by Baker & Taylor Publisher Services